S0-BSZ-669

The Lobsterman
and
the U.F.O.

The Lobsterman and the U.F.O.

Neal Parker

Camden, Maine

Published by Down East Books
A wholly owned subsidiary of The Rowman & Littlefield Publishing Group, Inc.
4501 Forbes Boulevard, Suite 200, Lanham, Maryland 20706
www.rowman.com

16 Carlisle Street, London W1D 3BT, United Kingdom

Distributed by NATIONAL BOOK NETWORK

Copyright © 2006 by Neal Evan Parker
First Down East Books edition published in 2014

This story is intended as a work of fiction. Any resemblance of the characters contained herein to persons living or dead, on this world or any other, is purely a coincidence.

All rights reserved. No part of this book may be reproduced in any form or by any electronic or mechanical means, including information storage and retrieval systems, without written permission from the publisher, except by a reviewer who may quote passages in a review.

British Library Cataloguing in Publication Information Available

Library of Congress Cataloging-in-Publication Data Available

ISBN 978-1-60893-350-1 (pbk. : alk. paper)—ISBN 978-1-60893-351-8 (electronic)

∞™ The paper used in this publication meets the minimum requirements of American National Standard for Information Sciences—Permanence of Paper for Printed Library Materials, ANSI/NISO Z39.48-1992.

Printed in the United States of America

For Annabel, now age four.
May you and your generation learn to appreciate the few
remaining Ralfs and Betsys of the world.
With love, Papa

Dear Reader...

It would be reasonable to suggest that most Americans know more about space aliens than they do about lobstermen. It is an assumption especially remarkable because though most people don't believe in beings from outer space, lobstermen are undeniable... and when sighted they can be at least as interesting. It is for that reason that the audience of this tale, while willing to accept the fanciful science contained herein, may be less equipped to understand the ways of the hardworking fisherman. Perhaps with this story that will change.

-N.E.P.
January 30, 2006
Rockland, Maine
The self-proclaimed "Lobster Capital of the World"

PART I

The Lobsterman and the U.F.O.

The Help Wanted sign smelled of bait even before
Ralf Winslow, lobsterman, tacked it to the side of
the dock house. "Sternman Wanted – Call 873-2..."
Ralf looked grudgingly at his handiwork. "Gettin' old;
puttin' that sign up." In fact he had put it up so many
times in recent months he carried it, with the tack, in
his pants pocket. "Just can't find a kid who wants to
shove dead fish into bait bags from sunrise to dark in
all sorts of weather."

Ralf took a look towards the mooring where his
hard-worn boat the *Betsy Ann Jolene* gently rolled.
Her bilge pump gave a few squirts, casting a greasy
rainbow upon the water. "Pump's keepin' up fine,"
Ralf thought to himself. Then he turned away and
headed for his truck and home.

Betsy Winslow, lobsterman's wife, had a fine meat-

3

loaf waiting on the table. Ralf sat down without a
word and pounded the overturned ketchup bottle
like patience wasn't a virtue. It was sometime during
his third bite that Ralf swallowed his mouthful
and grumbled, "You know if Ann and Jolene hadn't
got married I wouldn't be in this 'predictamint'.
My own girls run off and leave me to work the boat
alone... And my only grandson so undersized I
doubt Jolene even got her bait back." Betsy, for
whom the novelty of having her name on the stern
had long since waned, answered with a wave of her
fork, "If you weren't such a hard head Ralfie, maybe,
just maybe, someone would stick around a while!"

4

Ralf didn't bother to answer, or for that matter, listen.

The next morning, well before sunrise, Ralf Winslow threw some gear in his truck and with a tall cup of coffee placed sturdily between his knees, drove to the harbor. He was going fishing alone again. "Miserable hard work with eight hundred traps to haul and bait." Ralf thought unhappily. It was still dark as a pocket as he cast off the mooring to face a day he didn't much look forward to. Ralf heard Betsy's words ringing in his head, "You miserable old hake, it wouldn't hurt you to try and be nice." "Maybe," he caught himself saying aloud, "the wife is onto something."

To the east, morning stars slowly faded into a powder blue horizon. The fresh sea air began to put Ralf in an almost agreeable mood; the placid bay luring him into a short-lived calm as his boat glided towards his first string of traps.

The serenity ended when the crusty lobsterman was startled by a mystifying streak of light swooping across the dawn. The fiery white band closed with the surface of the water, tearing along the line of Ralf's traps and buoys. Before he could appreciate what was taking place, a steaming saucer the size of a kiddy park merry-go-round and just as colorful came to rest not twenty feet from crashing into the *Betsy Ann Jolene*.

Well, Ralf was in quite a fit about the loss of his

A steaming saucer came to rest not twenty feet away...

lobster gear. Too upset in fact to see an odd figure
exit the saucer and stumble into the water. When
Ralf saw the splash he came to his senses and
eased his boat in for a closer look. Then, realizing
he likely had the culprit who was responsible for cut-
ting up his gear, Ralf grabbed the long line stretching

6

from the stranger's suit with his boathook, tailed
it to his winch and reeled the scoundrel
aboard...

Ralf cussed up a storm as his unexpected guest
flopped onto the *Betsy Ann Jolene*'s deck, gained his
feet and reached to remove his helmet.

Four hands at the extremes of four arms unlocked the dark globe and lifted it away. Four eyes blinked in unison from an otherwise ordinary, even youthful face. One gander at this oddity left Ralf Winslow speechless... some might say for the first time in years. His mind worked feverishly to find the best way to react to the very unusual sight before him. At last, figuring out how to meet the stare of the strangers four eyes, Ralf declared, "You're Canadian, aren't you."

Ralf wasn't sure how, but he understood the stranger to reply, "Well you figured out I'm not from here and at least that's a start." Ralf didn't need to "figure out" much more. Instead, wasting no breath on formalities and with rare inspiration Ralf managed to solve an existing problem with the brilliant use of a new one. "You're right young fella', I don't much care where you come from. Still, as I see it, you owe me for a string of traps. And unless you have money hidden in that peculiar head to toe lifejacket of yours, I guess you are just going to have to work off the damage."

The stranger lifted one of his hands in protest but Ralf had the newcomer to the mat and threatened to call the harbormaster. That ended the objection so quickly that Ralf was fully convinced his newly acquired sternman was definitely not American.

Then came a loud gurgle and glug. Both Ralf and his reluctant shipmate turned to watch the saucer slip beneath the waves. "Don't worry about your jet boat, Mr. Bluenose (For Ralf, trying to be nice for a change, was sure that's what Canadians liked to be called) The water's not all that deep here and I can find that

infernal machine of yours again anyhow. Tell you what though, if you work the whole season I'll raise it back up for you and you can fix 'er in my barn."

And so over the next three months Ralf and Mr. Bluenose worked catchin' lobsters from the rolling deck of the *Betsy Ann Jolene*. From sunrise to sundown they worked at a feverish pace that other fishermen couldn't even hope to match. Of course the secret was in Mr. Bluenose's four hands. Simply, no one could empty and re-bait a trap faster and Ralf was pleased to get the work of two men for the price of one.

Word got out around Soft Shell Bay that old Ralf, the mysterious Mr. Bluenose and the *Betsy Ann Jolene* were having a highline summer; that is, making money hand over fist. Back home Betsy was answering the phone every hour from all sorts of people catching the scent of money and wanting to be Ralf's sternman, but of course the job was taken.

Betsy, not knowing why, noticed a change in Ralf. He began to whistle around the house, smiled sometimes and on one occasion gave Betsy a peck on the cheek for no reason whatsoever. He even promised his bride (he hadn't called her that since they got married) that at the end of the summer he would have enough money to buy himself a new truck and get Betsy a satellite television.

As for Mr. Bluenose, he lived in the woodshed and as per Ralf's instructions, kept a cap pulled well down over his topmost eyes. He also, when not working

From sunrise to sundown they worked at a feverish pace

11

traps, kept his extra arms tucked and hidden inside his orange bibs.

Ralf frequently reminded Mr. Bluenose that if he were "found out" the harbormaster would ship him back to Canada …and he certainly would not get his boat back.

Yet it was not the risk of capture that kept Mr. Bluenose working aboard the *Betsy Ann Jolene*. No, he had come to respect, even like the gruff Ralf Winslow. How could the alien, steeped in technology, not warm to a being who lived by wits, cunning and instinct? These traits were all too rare beyond the blue orb called Earth and to that end Mr. Bluenose even came to think of Ralf as a teacher. The saucer's crash had been unfortunate; but discovering a new world was why Mr. Bluenose had come visiting in the first place. His accident put him in the middle of a world he had only hoped to study from afar and with a human who, Bluenose came to realize, might well be the last of his kind.

Autumn came with storms that sang preludes of the coming winter. The *Betsy Ann Jolene* and her crew worked fewer and fewer traps until it was time to declare the season at an end.

Ralf and Mr. Bluenose had earned so much money that they went to Earl's New and Used Auto and each bought a brand-new pickup truck; the ultimate sign of a successful year. Then Mr. Bluenose did something special for Betsy. He had, in his spare time, constructed a satellite dish out of an old snow plow and a broken radio he found at a yard sale. Mr. Bluenose installed the dubious-looking contraption on the roof of the Winslow home. In short order a seemingly thrilled Mrs. Winslow politely chimed how good the reception had become and how very unusual the new channels were. Bluenose never expected Betsy to fully appreciate the devices unique capabilities.

With the lobstering all over, Ralf, good to his word, helped Mr. Bluenose raise his boat. When brought to the surface the saucer was covered with lobsters. It being off-season those lobsters fetched a handsome price and almost doubled what Ralf and Mr. Bluenose brought in the whole summer. They trailered the craft back to Ralf's barn where Mr. Bluenose worked round the clock repairing it, until late one night a wondrous blue glow crept out from between the barn boards. A

13

deep soothing hum from outside preceded a knock on
the Winslow door. When Ralf opened it, a look from
the other side told him it was time for Mr. Bluenose,
his friend, to go.

Together they slid back the large barn doors. The
saucer was pulsing, seemingly alive. Then Mr.
Bluenose pulled the hat from his head and threw off
his orange bibs. Ralf, not one prone to displays of
male bonding, offered a firm handshake goodbye. That
was not satisfactory for Mr. Bluenose, who wrapped

14

The saucer slipped from the barn...

his four arms around a stunned but eventually receptive Ralf. With farewells complete Mr. Bluenose jumped in his truck and drove up the ramp into his waiting saucer.

Then the light from the craft increased to that of a dozen suns and Ralf Winslow, lobsterman, had to cover his eyes. The saucer slipped from the barn heading ever skyward.

As the hum diminished Ralf opened his eyes in time to watch the saucer gain speed then vanish

15

amongst the stars. "Hmm, you know" Ralf said to no one in particular, "I suspect maybe that feller wasn't Canadian after all."

PART II

Invasion Earth

The lobster had lived quietly, mysteriously, for years untold on the ocean's floor. For countless spring moons the bottom-feeding cannibals marched as an army from the ocean depths to scavenge food close to shore. At summer's end they retreated to the vast dark sea. But one fateful year, nature lost her balance and the crustaceans did not retreat. Instead, they advanced shoreward... ready to overrun and eat humankind.

The first attack would be on the rocky coast of Maine where millions of their lobster kin had already given their lives. The dwellers of the deep, however, were not really in control of their depraved ambition. An unseen force was driving them to take their place in the new world order. A new Earth run by alien conquerors who had come from light years away...

Ralf Winslow, lobsterman, idled his boat the *Betsy Ann Jolene* ahead slow. With the wheel lashed to port the hard working craft slipped into a series of slow graceful circles. Ralf looked to the stern where his twelve-year-old grandson scoured the rails with brush and hose. The old man's affection for the boy didn't keep Ralf from snapping, "Get on with it. I'm not wasting a day's worth of gas doing loop de loops just 'cause it takes you so long to clean this here boat." Then Ralf continued under his breath, "And with us comin' in empty-handed again." That was true enough. No one could remember a worse season for lobstering.

Tim, daydreaming of video games, took another swig from his can of warm orange soda and scrubbed a little faster. Ten minutes later the *Betsy Ann Jolene* came to rest at her mooring in Soft Shell Bay.

"It's a lousy summer for lobsters, I'll tell you. Started slow and only got worse from there." Ralf grumbled, sitting on Betsy's couch.

"Ralfie, change outa those clothes... you're stinking up my slipcovers." answered his wife as she walked by with a big cardboard box. Ralf, unwilling to let go of a good tirade, didn't miss a beat, "Tell you what I think. Them critters are just eating my bait and sneaking away. Never seen anythin' like it. Catch is down to nothin'."

Betsy dropped a sizable empty carton at Ralf's feet. "That's right, and why we're having a yard sale. Got bills to pay, sweet-cheeks. Now fill this with your junk and when you're done fill another!" Ralf, knowing well Betsy had little appreciation for how he transformed complaining into a performance art, snapped up the box with a grunt and headed outside.

Ralf Winslow slid back the huge barn doors and peered to the dark within. He didn't like to come out there much anymore. Reminded him of his old friend Mr. Bluenose and Ralf didn't care to admit he missed him. "How long ago was that?" he thought. "Things were good around here for a while. Even thought my only grandson Tim might take to fishing like me. Instead he's turning all geeky like his father. Jolene never should have married that paper-pushing pencil neck." Ralf took a quick look over his shoulder to make sure no one heard his thoughts. Satisfied he was alone Ralf, dragged his empty box into the barn.

The timing of Ralf and Betsy's yard sale couldn't have been better. Set to coincide with Soft Shell Bay's Annual Lobster Jamboree, the town would be swarming with tourists. Since there was no lobster to steam in the World's Largest Cooker, the tourists, Ralf figured, would instead spend their money on any souvenir they could find, no matter how worthless.

For a week before the Jamboree, Ralf and Tim headed out mornings to "Feed the lobsters." as they liked to complain. Each afternoon when they got back they worked with Betsy on getting ready for the biggest yard sale Tariff County had ever seen. All kinds of busted lobster traps, pot buoys, radios, rusty stoves, kid's clothes and chipped dishes were stickered for the sale.

Very quickly the other fishermen of Soft Shell Bay, also in financial despair, caught on to the wisdom of Ralf and Betsy's yard sale. An impromptu meeting was held at the town dock. With some quarreling, bad language and name-calling the lobsterman decided to combine their efforts to have the biggest yard sale in all history; that being even bigger than the largest ever in Tariff County.

Ralf suggested the sale be held at the Jamboree grounds... in the eating tent where, this year, "r lobster would be eaten anyway." And Ralf ins

...decided to combine their efforts...

since the yard sale started as his idea, that his
tables be next to the World's Largest Lobster Cooker.
That prime sales location was right at the entrance
to the Jamboree. No one dared argue the point
with Ralf... more because he could talk longer and
louder than anyone and the Jamboree was only
two days away.

The next morning's peaceful sunrise was undis-
turbed by the usual sounds of oars, outboards and
un-muffled boat engines. Instead the new day was
introduced by the roar of pickup trucks and the
moan of belabored leaf-springs. The dump had opened
and the people of Soft Shell fought each other feverishly to supplement the trash they already had
to sell.

When the day of the Annual Lobster Jamboree
arrived Ralf had no need to duke it out at the dump. He
and Betsy owned two lifetimes worth of useless chattel

which they had already set up at the festival grounds. So early that morning Ralf decided to head down to the *Betsy Ann Jolene* to look in on her overburdened bilge pump. With the other lobstermen ashore it was oddly quiet in the harbor. So quiet and peaceful, in fact, that Ralf took a rare moment to laze aboard his boat.

Abruptly, Ralf's calm ended when a strange commotion in the water commanded his attention. The harbor's surface had churned to froth, causing Ralf to peer into the depths, seeking whatever invisible thing might be at work.

What Ralf couldn't have known was that the lobsters, by destroying all the traps, had fired the opening salvo of their invasion. Had Ralf been aware that a great attack was about to take place he might have tried to give alarm. Nor was anyone else on earth alert to the fleet of menacing spacecraft that circled above the cloud-covered Soft Shell Bay.

While the ravenous lobsters edged hungrily toward shore, the local lobstermen were actually faced with a different invasion of sorts. A large protest had gathered at the beach adjacent to the fair grounds. The group of vigilantes called themselves S.E.L.T.O., which stood for Stop Eating Living Things Okay? Every year they assembled from all over the country to disrupt the Lobster Jamboree. One year a half dozen of the radicals handcuffed themselves to the World's Largest Lobster Cooker. That didn't stop an unsympathetic Ralf from turning on the gas and lighting the fire. In short order those overheated S.E.L.T.O. people were scrambling for their keys. Now the protesters stood by the sea, locked arm in arm, holding banners and singing in chorus, "We shall overcome..."

Ralf, eyeing the demonstration from the *Betsy Ann Jolene*, jumped into his skiff and pulled for the beach. Protesters or not, Ralf was not going to deal with the Jamboree traffic. It was far easier to row to the fair grounds and push his way on foot through the "sissy lobster sympathizers." As he landed his rowboat and muscled it up the shore, the sight of the huffing purple-faced lobsterman parted the protesters much the way Moses parted the Red Sea. With his skiff secured Ralf acknowledged the S.E.L.T.O folks with a teeth-baring growl. Certain the "lobster-lovers" wouldn't dare mess with his boat, Ralf chuckled and marched off singing, "We shall overeat..."

When Ralf was out of reach the "lobster-lovers" hurled a torrent of insults at the "big bad lobsterman." Had they remained silent a short while longer the protesters might have heard the skitter-scatter of hungry lobsters approaching from just below the tide line.

Three hundred yards up the shore later, Ralf joined Betsy and Tim by the World's Largest Cooker; their yard sale tables well stacked with overpriced collectables. Under the eating tent and sprawled across the fair grounds other fishermen's families displayed their goods. What couldn't fit on the tables in plain view was waiting beneath, crammed into swelled boxes.

Ralf chuckled and marched off singing...

Between the Cooker and Betsy's goods stood an odd-looking device. It was a fancy wood cabinet full of dials, tubes and wire. The thickest wire ran to a rusty snow plow. Winding the other way was a set of jumper cables clamped to a greasy car battery. The whole device was nicely bound with silver cloth tape. Its appearance at the yard sale was cause of a serious dispute between Ralf and his missus. Ralf argued that the satellite receiver Mr. Bluenose had made Betsy still worked perfectly fine. But Betsy was tired of foreign movies and got herself hooked up to cable instead.

At last the time had come to officially commence Soft Shell Bay's Annual Lobster Jamboree. Word had gone out to the media about the lack of lobsters being offset by the abundance of "quality" yard sale items. It was a human interest story that had reporters climbing all over each other. It may be for that reason the crowd waiting to get into the Jamboree was of historic proportion.

At eleven a.m. the local fire trucks wailed their sirens and the previous year's Claw Princess cut the ceremonial ribbon. With the gates open, thirty thousand souvenir-hungry tourists thronged ahead. As they did the clouds over Soft Shell Bay tore apart with a thunderous roar. Above the frightened masses hovered not less than a hundred spacecraft. They were ugly barnacle-shaped creations with mouths facing downward. No sooner had the spacecraft revealed themselves than blood-curdling screams came from

The clouds tore apart with a thunderous roar!

the beach. The cries for help were quickly subdued by the ravenous lobsters. Too late The S.E.L.T.O. folks realized they had taken the wrong side.

Then the lobsters advanced en masse, their skitter-scatter so deafeningly loud and painful it overwhelmed all other human senses. Ten million pounds of blood-thirsty crustaceans fanned out and headed for the main part of their barbaric feast; their mindless bodies directed by the spaceships above.

Ralf, who was extremely well practiced in turning deaf to that which he cared not to hear, was the only human who was not passed out from the deadly cacophony. He didn't know for certain what was going on, but he was quite sure that something was interrupting his yard sale. Ralf, frustrated, expressed himself in the only way that made sense to him at that particular moment. He pounded his fist atop Mr. Bluenose's satellite machine.

The jolt of Ralf's powerfully clenched hand was so hard it triggered a concealed switch at the back of the wooden box. Suddenly a mechanism Bluenose had placed within Betsy's satellite receiver sprang to life. The jumper cables sparked and the contraption began to wheeze. The usually unflappable lobstermen jumped back as a shaft of red light shot upward from the device's rusty plow. A thousand feet up the beam reached its apex and curved downward to the sea. The red light broadened into a majestic rainbow that seemed to emanate from the World's Largest Lobster Cooker itself...

Before anyone else got eaten, the lobsters changed course. They lined up in formation and seeking the rainbows end, headed straight for the cooker. Ralf didn't have to be told to turn on the gas and light 'er up. Somehow the critters were climbing up the cooker and throwing themselves in like lemmings.

Overhead the foiled invaders had not escaped the ill effects of even a short stay in the earth's atmosphere.

While Ralf gloated at his highline catch, an unplugged clock radio on a nearby table came crackling to life. The space ships above were attempting to communicate. A rasping voice inquired, "Um, how much for the dresser? Is that real Chippendale?" A hundred feet away a broken television demanded, "Five bucks for the Mickey watch... not a penny more!"

Soon every used radio, T V and record player was calling out: all trying to buy, cheat and swap the junk at the World's Largest Yard Sale. Even an ancient gramophone started to churn out a bid on itself but that was just too scratchy for Ralf to understand.

By the time thirty thousand tourists, reporters and lobstermen regained consciousness Ralf had negotiated away most everything at the yard sale. Most everything except for a large collection of eight track tapes... And, needless to say, Ralf held on to Mr. Bluenose's contraption. The spaceships, loaded to the gills, had staggered skyward. Laden as they were many foundered and burned up while falling back into the earth's atmosphere.

Because everyone for miles around was passed out and because Ralf was the only witness, no one really knew what happened. Ralf didn't try too hard to figure it out either. During the three-day Jamboree he had caught and sold over ten million pounds of lobster. Ralf Winslow was now a rich man. What is more, the S.E.L.T.O. folks had mysteriously disappeared. Ralf, pleased with the recent turn of events, knew better than to look his gift horse in the mouth.

PART III

The Immortal Lobsterman

Ralf Winslow, lobsterman, did not remain wealthy for long. Perhaps he was never meant to be prosperous in a way that could readily be noted by others. No sooner did Ralf place his fortune in the bank than he was approached with an investment opportunity that promised him a page in history. Unfortunately the freshwater lobster farm in Nigeria was an immediate bust. Ralf never saw his partners or his money again.

Meanwhile, galaxies away, the news of Ralf's defeat of the Earth invaders was so well received that Ralf had become something of a celebrity. And nowhere was he regarded more highly than on the very planet Mr. Bluenose called home. It was decided by the leaders on that world it was time for Ralf and his old friend to meet again...

Ralf Winslow, lobsterman, muckled another trap up onto the rail of the *Betsy Ann Jolene.* Its only yield, three starfish, a sea cucumber and one undersized lobster. Ralf tossed the useless lot overboard, re-baited his trap and heaved it off the stern. The old fisherman was more inconsolable than ever. He had won then lost a great fortune.

To Ralf's thinking, it wasn't enough that he had been fishing for forty-five years. God had granted him the health and unfortunately the necessity to go it another forty-five. The lobsterman shook his fist at the cold gray sky and bellowed, "You're a miserable sadistic bugger!" Then with a twinge of guilt and the realization he still had more to lose, Ralf looked up again and added more reverently, "Jus' seeing if you're really payin' attention."

Back home, Betsy, hardly surprised at Ralf's foolish investment, wasn't completely disappointed the money was gone. "Too much change at my age," She confided to her daughters. A confession not well received by her girls, nor their "good for nothin' husbands." as Ralf often referred to them.

It being a Sunday in June and a foggy one at that, Ralf decided to stay in and keep his missus company. Since he could no longer afford to pay for Betsy's five hundred cable channels, Ralf figured he could at

least comfort the wife with his fine companionship
once in a while.

So when breakfast was over Ralf licked the bacon
grease from his fingers, sat back and stared past the
window into the fog. Betsy brought the dishes to the
sink and ran the hot water until it actually was.

"Fog's pretty thick." tried Ralf at some small talk.
"Sure is." said a grudgingly responsive Betsy. For five
minutes Ralf leaned back, looked out the smudged
glass and drummed his knurled fingers on the table.
Betsy, hanging her wet dishrag on the oven door han-
dle, turned to her husband. "Ralf, don't sit there for
my sake. I'll love you just as much if you were some-
where else!" Ralf, not needing to be told twice, jumped
up, gave his wife a grateful look and hurried away.

Four hours later, Ralf, having consumed a substantial quantity of coffee, sugar and cream at the Towne Diner, headed home. Turning into his long dirt driveway the fog was so thick Ralf had to run the windshield wipers just to see them. Moments later the barn's translucent shadow loomed ahead. "That's odd." Ralf said aloud, applying his brakes. Odd indeed, for Ralf never left the barn doors open.

The lobsterman cautiously stepped from his pickup, then froze as he detected the clamor of an intruder inside the barn. Despite his advancing years Ralf instinctively braced himself, fists clenched, ready for battle, while his startled nerves used every other muscle to keep his four hours of coffee from causing embarrassment. In short order a figure emerged from the barn's depths. Ralf, poised for a fight, suddenly did a complete turnabout, breaking into a spontaneous dance of joy. Standing before him in orange bibs and ski-cap was his long-lost friend... and possibly his savior.

"Mr. Bluenose! Mr. Bluenose!" sang out Ralf, hugging the welcome visitor into a whirling jig. Though Bluenose never spoke aloud he let the lobsterman know he was overjoyed as well. As Ralf waltzed Mr. Bluenose into the house to show Betsy the good news, his less virtuous self hoped his foreign friend was not just back for a social call. To that end the lobsterman should not be judged too harshly.

"Mr. Bluenose! Mr. Bluenose!" sang out Ralf...

Betsy was a fine hostess that afternoon. She put on a pot of tea and sat quietly in her place as the two "men" caught up on old times. Betsy, shrewder than Ralf ever appreciated, suspected rightfully this sudden visit was not without purpose. And though Mr. Bluenose had a strange way of talking without moving his lips, Betsy was able to follow every word. She even remained gracious when Mr. Bluenose licked the glaze from his teacup and declared it the best frosting he had ever tasted.

Betsy could also make her thoughts known without saying a word. So when Mr. Bluenose let the cat out of the bag and asked Ralf to sign some papers accepting a highly prized honorarium, Betsy gave her husband a look which he clearly understood, "You ain't signing nothin' without a lawyer!" Ralf, unwilling to argue the point, saved his manhood by suggesting that he and Mr. Bluenose continue their conversation back at the Towne Diner.

In a private corner booth at Ralf's home away from home Mr. Bluenose tried to explain the award his superiors had instructed him to bring to the hero lobsterman. Telepathy is not as exacting as readers of science fiction have been led to believe. Therefore, with such a huge cultural gap between Mr. Bluenose and Ralf, the space traveler's accent was, at times, a little hard to understand... "You're going to use my what for a what?" asked a very confused Ralf.

It would not be fair to Ralf to say he didn't know what he was signing. He certainty understood that Mr. Bluenose had never done him wrong before. And besides, how could he go wrong when he was promised something for nothing? Ralf was also keenly aware that by signing the papers against Betsy's wishes he was reaffirming his power as lord of his castle.

Now all that remained was for Ralf to inform his missus about his recent doings... a job he shortly realized with some fear he didn't care to do. Would Betsy be pleased that Mr. Bluenose simply wanted to use his likeness, that is to say, Ralf's picture, and for that he would receive some kind of prize? And if Mr. Bluenose's people, whoever they were, wanted to present Ralf with some kind of lobstering trophy, why not? These thoughts spun wildly in Ralf's mind as he drove home in the unrelenting fog. Mr. Bluenose sat quietly beside him, listening in on Ralf's confused musings. The alien smiled to himself, aware his friend had no idea just how famous he was about to become.

Arriving home, Betsy's reaction was not one Ralf had prepared himself for. The good woman listened, stared, then said nothing before turning away.

The thick fog continued day after wretched day, obscuring anything beyond an arm's length. The gray wet veil did not keep Ralf from working his traps. Besides, for Ralf, going fishing was a welcome chance to avoid his wife's punishing silence. So each morning the tired lobsterman headed out in the *Betsy Ann Jolene* with nothing but an old compass and his crumpled chart guiding him to his catch. Fishing was hard enough when you could see, but with the blinding fog, each exhausting trip felt like the work of ten.

Mr. Bluenose, out of concern for his overly tired friend, offered to make some modern additions to the *Betsy Ann Jolene*. However, Ralf, proudly set in his ways, would have no part of it. "Doubt any silly electrical arcade games can tell me where the lobsters are!"

But when Ralf's grandson Tim came to stay for the July Fourth weekend the old lobsterman had a change of heart. The insensible teenager had no inter-est in anything anymore but sitting in front of one video screen or another playing shoot this and catch that. Ralf, sensing it was his last chance to see a fifth generation of Winslow lobsterman, finally conceded he needed Mr. Bluenose. "Have at it. You put as many of your television contraptions on my boat as you please. Just make it so that boy wants to go fishing." The poor lobsterman's emotion was so genuine Mr. Bluenose determined his friend would not be disappointed.

It is not that Mr. Bluenose didn't already have his hands full. He was working against the clock to prepare Ralf's honorarium. Mr. Bluenose just knew the timing was also perfect to answer his friend's call.

Sparing not a moment following the lobsterman's request, Mr. Bluenose marched into Betsy's living room. Taking a page from "Ralf's Book of Abrupt Behavior", Bluenose threw Tim's lazy feet off the end table. He then grabbed the Game Boy controls from the grandson's hand while ripping the wire from the television. A second later Bluenose was out the door and headed for the barn; the riled teenager chasing close behind with shouts of "Hey you creep..." and an explosion of slang that stopped as quickly as it had begun. Tim was in the barn. Before him, waiting in the gangway of his glowing space saucer, was the four-eyed, four-armed Mr. Bluenose.

The next morning, coffee in hand, Ralf headed down to the harbor. It was the Fourth of July but Ralf was in no mood to mark any special occasions. There were still traps to check and Betsy's silence to steer

Waiting in the gangway
was the four eyed, four armed Mr. Bluenose.

clear of. Then there was his grandson Tim to not think about. And Ralf wondered why he should be in such a dither about the boy. "He's not a real Winslow anyway... nothing but the spawn of the 'good for nothing' Jolene married."

Ralf shuddered at his own train of thought. "Maybe it's the fog talking. Haven't seen past my nose in weeks." The lobsterman threw the oars in his skiff and rowed blindly through the moorings to where he knew the *Betsy Ann Jolene* should be... but wasn't.

The first thing Ralf did when he noticed his boat missing was to peer beneath the waves. Past experience had told him, if the boat isn't where you left it, there is a good chance it is below where you left it. His attempt to find his boat resting on the murky bottom having proved fruitless, Ralf's blood began to boil. He rose, legs astride his skiff and, erupting like a volcano, the embittered lobsterman shook both fists at the fog-obscured heavens. Ralf, completely enraged, was about to let forth a string of oaths that would have embarrassed the king of the underworld when suddenly he heard the chuga-chug-glub of a familiar diesel. It grew louder and louder until an unseen voice called, "Hey grandpa, could you pass up that mooring line?"

A minute later the *Betsy Ann Jolene* hove in view. At the helm, which was now a joystick, was Tim. On the bow, ready to take the mooring from Ralf, was Mr. Bluenose, grinning from ear to ear.

Ralf threw the slime covered line to Bluenose. Then with the grace of someone who has made the same jump all too often, Ralf, gazelle like, leapt from his skiff to the aft deck of his lobster boat. Landing with a muffled clump, Ralf beheld a glowing specter before him. Radiant against the fog-draped boat and placed all around the wheelhouse were ten ham-can-sized video screens. Some were red. Some blue. Three had lines that swept in circles while still others had rolling maps with pictures of fish and boats. All the screens were emblazoned with numbers that changed and flashed every time the boat rolled or a seagull flew by. Across the *Betsy Ann Jolene's* cabin top was an array of antennas and dishes and humming things that whirled searchingly above and below. Ralf had not seen anything like it since the time he tried to buy batteries at Radio Shack around Christmas.

Nearly hypnotized, Ralf just stood and stared while Tim explained. "Didn't want to make you think your boat got stole, grandpa. It's just that your friend Mr. Bluenose figured we should do a shakedown cruise before you got here." Then Ralf, coming to his senses, threw Mr. Bluenose an approving glance while Tim, rarely gregarious, continued, "we got forward-rear-bottom and side-scanning sonar. There's dual interfacing satellite and radar navigation systems with environmental sensors to calibrate... " It was all Greek to Ralf. All that mattered was that his grandson Tim was on the boat.

"Come on Grandpa Ralf, let's go catch us some lobsters!" Ralf Winslow, always master of his vessel quickly re-established the chain of command. "Now hold on a second. Still don't see no contraption here that'll put bait on this here boat."

Shortly after, the *Betsy Ann Jolene* was dockside, loading a hefty sum of rotting bait fish. With the boat laden, fueled up and ready for a day's work, Ralf and Mr. Bluenose cast off while Tim used his new toys to set the course. Uneasy with all the strange equipment aboard, Ralf peered suspiciously over Tim's shoulder. Then Ralf, studying one of the screens, went to the rail and sang out through the fogbound moorings, "Hey! Bernard! Your fly is open." After that Ralf relaxed, perched himself on the engine box and sipped his now cold coffee.

The *Betsey Ann Jolene* was rounding into the

wind to pick up another fogbound trap when Mr. Bluenose announced (telepathically) that he had work to do on shore in regards to the July Fourth fireworks. Ralf, aware of just how far from home they were, protested, "Come on now Mr. Bluenose. We can't drop what we're doin' just to get you back to town. Besides, fog hasn't let up in weeks. Won't be any sky show tonight..." Mr. Bluenose then shed his cap and orange bibs. His eyes sparkled in response, "Don't worry Ralf I can find my own way back. And just wait until tonight. There is going to be quite the show!"

With that Bluenose whistled between his thumb and forefinger. The sea boiled around the *Betsy Ann Jolene* while there arose, close astern, Mr. Bluenose's space saucer. With a quick leap across the water Mr. Bluenose and his craft were gone.

Ralf and Tim didn't discuss Mr. Bluenose's unusual exit. It is possible that each felt they were protecting Mr. Bluenose's privacy. Whatever the reason, instead of bringing up the strange event, they turned to lobstering with a newly discovered passion.

It was just before midday when, without warning, the newfangled antenna array ceased all movement and all ten video screens began to sputter and smoke. Then the familiar, reassuring sound of chuga-chug-glub tapered away to silence. The once lively *Betsy Ann Jolene* was dead in the water.

Ralf's verbal abuse against anything invented after the wheel was one of the most original the confused Tim or anyone could have hoped to hear. The whole situation was so interesting in fact that, for the first time since reaching his teens, Tim was attentive after a video screen had gone blank. Then Ralf, barking at the boy, yanked him from his role as spectator.

"Where the heck is my compass?!"

Tim was dumbstruck long enough for his grandfather to expound some more... "You know, the round thing that shows where north is! And the chart ...made of paper, like a map?" The boy remarkably

The sea boiled around the Betsy Ann Jolene.

found his tongue. "We took those off the boat. Mr.
Bluenose said you didn't need 'em."

Ralf had a few choice words for Mr. Bluenose,
which he muttered under his breath out of respect
for Tim's youth. Then Ralf, without provocation,
did something extraordinary... he calmed down...
grew quiet. Taking in a lungful of Zen filled sea
air Ralf turned to his grandson, "Looky here Tim.
Here's what we got to do. . ." Together they dragged
a monstrous size battery right up close to the
engine. With some old pliers and a rusty knife
Ralf showed Tim how to hotwire the starter. With a

string for the throttle and a kick to the gearbox the *Betsy Ann Jolene* was again a moving, living thing. Ralf, having jammed a pipe wrench atop the rudder stock (for there was no other way to steer), turned the boat so the deep rolling waves were almost at his back. On course at last the lobsterman shouted above the throbbing engine to his awestruck grandson, "Wind's been east for two weeks. These rollers are headed west toward land. You get up to the bow... away from the exhaust. When you smell the worst stink in the world let me know. That'll be Egg Rock where the birds roost. Whole damn thing's covered with gull poop. After you catch your nose full we'll steer more to the south'rd."

In that way and using a few other old fishermen's tricks Ralf navigated his boat through the blinding fog safely back to Soft Shell Bay. With every wave that rolled beneath them Tim's admiration for his antiquated grandfather immeasurably grew.

After tying the *Betsy Ann Jolene* to her mooring, Ralf and Tim rowed straight for the beach. A crowd had gathered for the July Fourth barbeque. Betsy was there dressing chicken wings and catty chatting with her neighbors. Ralf and his grandson approached through the crowd, the old man's arm wrapped across the boy's shoulder. It was a moment so full of warmth and out of character for the two of them that Betsy finally broke her silence to her husband with a curious "Hello Ralfie."

It was a splendid picnic. So delightful a time was had that folks were ready to forgive the fog which was responsible for calling off the fireworks. But then at the appointed hour, as though a switch had been thrown, the sky miraculously cleared. At the same time a saucer-shaped rocket jetted skyward followed by a trail of intensifying colors and stars. The crowd gasped at the noisy spectacle overhead. With the fog gone, a backdrop of heavenly stars and planets joined in chorus. It was the first night sky anyone had enjoyed since the long fog set in.

Ralf, Betsy and Tim stood amidst their friends and neighbors delighting in the finest Forth of July display

Soft Shell had ever witnessed. Ralf, tickled by the fire-works caught himself thinking, "Mr. Bluenose sure can put on a show." Then the smiling lobsterman was struck with a great revelation... "Bluenose would never build something that got broke. Those electric contraptions on the boat were made to self destruct!" Amidst the hubbub overhead Ralf peered down at the young Winslow standing by his side. "Maybe he'll be a lobsterman after all." the old fisherman chuckled to himself.

Suddenly the crowed cheered as the entire sky seemed to explode. Ralf looked up in time to witness a strange vision. Standing large above the Milky Way was a muscled warrior with the body of a beast. The celestial creature bore a spear in one hand and a dead twenty-pound lobster in the other. More extraordinary still was that the face of this mythic being possessed an uncanny likeness to Soft Shell's very own Ralf Winslow, lobsterman.

The crowed cheered in deafening recognition. Betsy yelled in Ralf's ear, "See you old fart, money ain't everything." Tim jumped and yelled with the best of them. Then, as the smoke cleared, eight of the fiery stars sped away and established themselves in the night sky. With that the legend of Ralf Winslow was immortalized.

When the three Winslows got home later that night Betsy headed for the back door while Ralf and Tim peeked into the barn. As expected, Mr. Bluenose was

Ralf looked up in time to witness a strange vision.

53

gone. Above them the stars shone joyously.

Walking to the house it was Tim who broke the silence. "Grandpa, I gotta tell you. Mr. Bluenose is *not* from Canada." Ralf, surprised by the comment, winked with his grumbled reply, "Do you think me such a pea brain Tim not to know a New Yorker when I sees one!?"

THE END

Captain Neal Evan Parker was born in Brooklyn New York in 1956. While sailing the waters of New England as a teenager, Neal became devoted to traditional sailing vessels. By the age of 20 he was a licensed captain. Since then Parker has skippered over a dozen schooners and traditional craft. In 1986 Captain Parker purchased and restored the 67-foot schooner *Wendameen.* Dedicating four years to her restoration, he placed the schooner into the Maine windjammer business. In April 2005 after a run of almost 20 years Capt. Neal Parker sold his beloved vessel. With several books published and more on the way he is now devoting his time to professional ship model work, writing and being a full time father.

Artist Jim Sollers is a native of Maryland who has called Maine his home for untold years. Originally trained in fine arts, Jim is sought after as both a fine artist and illustrator specializing in marine themes. More recently Mr. Sollers has garnered acclaim for his artwork in nature books and children's stories. In the world of fine art his paintings are highly prized in private collections in the U.S. and abroad. Well read and a fan of classic science fiction art, Jim Sollers brings to The Lobsterman and the U.F.O. both his talent and enthusiasm. His pen has breathed life into the world of Ralf Winslow.